D1765062

THE SINS OF PRINCE SARADINE

G.K. Chesterton

first published in

1910

When Flambeau took his month's holiday from his office in Westminster he took it in a small sailing-boat, so small that it passed much of its time as a rowing-boat. He took it, moreover, in little rivers in the Eastern counties, rivers so small that the boat looked like a magic boat, sailing on land through meadows and cornfields. The vessel was just comfortable for two people; there was room only for necessities, and Flambeau had stocked it with such things as his special philosophy considered necessary. They reduced themselves, apparently, to four essentials: tins of salmon, if he should want to eat;

loaded revolvers, if he should want to fight; a bottle of brandy, presumably in case he should faint; and a priest, presumably in case he should die. With this light luggage he crawled down the little Norfolk rivers, intending to reach the Broads at last, but meanwhile delighting in the overhanging gardens and meadows, the mirrored mansions or villages, lingering to fish in the pools and corners, and in some sense hugging the shore.

Like a true philosopher, Flambeau had no aim in his holiday; but, like a true philosopher, he had an excuse. He had a sort of half purpose, which he took just so seriously that its success would crown the holiday, but just so lightly that its failure would not spoil it. Years ago, when he had been a king of thieves and the most famous figure in Paris, he had often received wild communications of approval, denunciation, or even love; but one had, somehow, stuck in his memory. It consisted simply of a visiting-card, in an envelope with an English postmark. On the back of the card was written in French and in green ink: "If you ever retire and become respectable, come and see me. I want to meet you, for I have met all the other great men of my time. That trick of yours of getting one detective to arrest the other was the most splendid scene in French history." On the front of the card was engraved in the formal fashion, "Prince Saradine, Reed House, Reed Island, Norfolk."

He had not troubled much about the prince then, beyond

ascertaining that he had been a brilliant and fashionable figure in southern Italy. In his youth, it was said, he had eloped with a married woman of high rank; the escapade was scarcely startling in his social world, but it had clung to men's minds because of an additional tragedy: the alleged suicide of the insulted husband, who appeared to have flung himself over a precipice in Sicily. The prince then lived in Vienna for a time, but his more recent years seemed to have been passed in perpetual and restless travel. But when Flambeau, like the prince himself, had left European celebrity and settled in England, it occurred to him that he might pay a surprise visit to this eminent exile in the Norfolk Broads. Whether he should find the place he had no idea; and, indeed, it was sufficiently small and forgotten. But, as things fell out, he found it much sooner than he expected.

They had moored their boat one night

under a bank veiled
in high grasses and
short pollarded trees.
Sleep, after heavy
sculling, had come
to them early, and
by a corresponding
accident they awoke
before it was light. To
speak more strictly,
they awoke before
it was daylight; for
a large lemon moon
was only just setting
in the forest of high
grass above their

heads, and the sky was of a vivid violet-blue, nocturnal but bright. Both men had simultaneously a reminiscence of childhood, of the elfin and adventurous time when tall weeds close over us like woods. Standing up thus against the large low moon, the daisies really seemed to be giant daisies, the dandelions to be giant dandelions. Somehow it reminded them of the dado of a nursery wall-paper. The drop of the river-bed sufficed to sink them under the roots of all shrubs and flowers and make them gaze upwards at the grass. "By Jove!" said Flambeau, "it's like being in fairyland."

Father Brown sat bolt

upright in the boat and crossed himself. His movement was so abrupt that his friend asked him, with a mild stare, what was the matter.

"The people who wrote the mediaeval ballads," answered the priest, "knew more about fairies than you do. It isn't only nice things that happen in fairyland."

"Oh, bosh!" said Flambeau. "Only nice things could happen under such an innocent moon. I am for pushing on now and seeing what does really come. We may die and rot before we ever see again such a moon or such a mood."

"All right," said Father Brown. "I never said it was

always wrong to enter fairyland. I only said it was always dangerous."

They pushed slowly up the brightening river; the glowing violet of the sky and the pale gold of the moon grew fainter and fainter, and faded into that vast colourless cosmos that precedes the colours of the dawn.

When the first faint stripes of red and gold and grey split the horizon from end to end they were broken by the black bulk of a town or village which sat on the river just ahead of them. It was already an easy twilight, in which all things were visible, when they came under the hanging roofs and bridges of this riverside hamlet. The houses, with their long, low, stooping roofs, seemed to come down to drink at the river, like huge grey and red cattle. The broadening and whitening dawn had already turned to working daylight before they saw any living creature on the wharves and bridges of that silent town.

Eventually they saw a very placid and prosperous man in his shirt sleeves, with a face as round as the recently sunken moon, and rays of red whisker around the low arc of it, who was leaning on a post above the sluggish tide. By an impulse not to be analysed, Flambeau rose to his full height in the swaying boat and shouted at the man to ask if he knew Reed Island or Reed House. The prosperous man's smile grew slightly more expansive, and he simply pointed up the river towards the next bend of it. Flambeau went ahead without further speech.

The boat took many such grassy corners

and followed many
such reedy and silent
reaches of river; but
before the search had
become monotonous
they had swung
round a specially
sharp angle and come
into the silence of
a sort of pool or
lake, the sight of
which instinctively
arrested them. For
in the middle of this
wider piece of water,
fringed on every

side with rushes, lay a long, low islet, along which ran a long, low house or bungalow built of bamboo or some kind of tough tropic cane. The upstanding rods of bamboo which made the walls were pale yellow, the sloping rods that made the roof were of darker red or brown, otherwise the long house was a thing of repetition and monotony. The early morning breeze rustled the reeds round the island and sang in the strange ribbed house as in a giant pan-pipe.

"By George!" cried Flambeau; "here is the place, after all! Here is Reed Island, if ever there was one. Here is Reed House, if it is anywhere. I believe that fat man with whiskers was a fairy."

"Perhaps," remarked Father Brown impartially. "If he was, he was a bad fairy."

But even as he spoke the impetuous Flambeau had run his boat ashore in the rattling reeds, and they stood in the long, quaint islet beside the odd and silent house.

The house stood with its back, as it were, to the river and the only landing-stage; the main entrance was on the other side, and looked down the long island garden. The visitors approached it, therefore, by a small path running round nearly three sides of the house, close under the low eaves. Through three different windows on three different sides they looked in on the same long, well-lit room, panelled in light wood, with a large number of looking-glasses, and laid out as for an elegant lunch. The front door, when they came round to it at last, was flanked by two turquoise-blue flower pots. It was opened by a butler of the drearier type— long, lean, grey and listless—who murmured that Prince Saradine was from home at present, but was expected hourly; the house being kept ready for him and his guests. The exhibition of the card with the scrawl of green ink awoke a flicker of life in the parchment face of the depressed retainer, and it was with a certain shaky courtesy that he suggested that the strangers should remain. "His Highness may be here any minute," he said, "and would be distressed to have just missed any gentleman he had invited. We have orders always to keep a little cold lunch for him and his friends, and I am sure he would wish it to be offered."

Moved with curiosity to this minor adventure, Flambeau assented gracefully, and followed the old man, who ushered him ceremoniously into the long, lightly panelled room. There

was nothing very
notable about it,
except the rather
unusual alternation
of many long, low
windows with many
long, low oblongs of
looking-glass, which
gave a singular air
of lightness and
unsubstantialness
to the place. It
was somehow like
lunching out of
doors. One or two
pictures of a quiet

kind hung in the corners, one a large grey photograph of a very young man in uniform, another a red chalk sketch of two long-haired boys. Asked by Flambeau whether the soldierly person was the prince, the butler answered shortly in the negative; it was the prince's younger brother, Captain Stephen Saradine, he said. And with that the old man seemed to dry up suddenly and lose all taste for conversation.

After lunch had tailed off with exquisite coffee and liqueurs, the guests were introduced to the garden, the library, and the housekeeper—a dark, handsome lady, of no little majesty, and rather like a plutonic Madonna. It appeared that she and the butler were the only survivors of the prince's original foreign menage the other servants now in the house being new and collected in Norfolk by the housekeeper. This latter lady went by the name of Mrs. Anthony, but she spoke with a slight

Italian accent, and Flambeau did not doubt that Anthony was a Norfolk version of some more Latin name. Mr. Paul, the butler, also had a faintly foreign air, but he was in tongue and training English, as are many of the most polished men-servants of the cosmopolitan nobility.

Pretty and unique

as it was, the place had about it a curious luminous sadness. Hours passed in it like days. The long, well-windowed rooms were full of daylight, but it seemed a dead daylight. And through all other incidental noises, the sound of talk, the clink of glasses, or the passing feet of servants, they could hear on all sides of the house the melancholy noise of the river.

"We have taken a wrong turning, and come to a wrong place," said Father Brown, looking out of the window at the grey-green sedges and the silver flood. "Never mind; one can sometimes do good by being the right person in the wrong place."

Father Brown, though commonly a silent, was an oddly sympathetic little man, and in those few but endless hours he unconsciously sank deeper into the secrets of Reed House than his professional friend. He had that knack of friendly silence which is so essential to gossip; and saying scarcely a word, he probably obtained from his new acquaintances all that in any case they would have told. The butler indeed was naturally uncommunicative. He betrayed a sullen and almost animal affection for his master; who, he said, had been very badly treated. The chief

offender seemed
to be his highness's
brother, whose name
alone would lengthen
the old man's lantern
jaws and pucker
his parrot nose into
a sneer. Captain
Stephen was a ne'er-
do-well, apparently,
and had drained his
benevolent brother
of hundreds and
thousands; forced
him to fly from
fashionable life and

live quietly in this retreat. That was all Paul, the butler, would say, and Paul was obviously a partisan.

The Italian housekeeper was somewhat more communicative, being, as Brown fancied, somewhat less content. Her tone about her master was faintly acid; though not without a certain awe. Flambeau and his friend were standing in the room of the looking-glasses examining the red sketch of the two boys, when the housekeeper swept in swiftly on some domestic errand. It was a peculiarity of this glittering, glass-panelled place that anyone entering was reflected in four or five mirrors at once; and Father Brown, without turning round, stopped in the middle of a sentence of family criticism. But Flambeau, who had his face close up to the picture, was already saying in a loud voice, "The brothers Saradine, I suppose. They both look innocent enough. It would be hard to say which is the good brother and which the bad." Then, realising the lady's presence, he turned the conversation with some triviality, and strolled out into the garden. But Father Brown still gazed steadily at the red crayon sketch; and Mrs. Anthony still gazed steadily at Father Brown.

She had large and tragic brown eyes, and her olive face glowed darkly with a curious and painful wonder—as of one doubtful of a stranger's identity or purpose. Whether the little priest's coat and creed touched some southern memories of confession, or whether she fancied he knew more than he did, she said to him in a low voice as to a fellow plotter, "He is right enough in one way, your friend. He says it would be hard to pick out the good and bad brothers. Oh, it would be hard, it would be mighty hard, to pick out the good one."

"I don't understand you," said Father Brown, and began to

move away.

The woman took a step nearer to him, with thunderous brows and a sort of savage stoop, like a bull lowering his horns.

"There isn't a good one," she hissed. "There was badness enough in the captain taking all that money, but I don't think there was much goodness in the prince giving it. The captain's not the only one with something against him."

A light dawned on the cleric's averted face, and his mouth formed silently the word "blackmail." Even as he did so the woman turned an abrupt white face over her shoulder and almost fell. The

door had opened
soundlessly and the
pale Paul stood like a
ghost in the doorway.
By the weird trick
of the reflecting
walls, it seemed
as if five Pauls had
entered by five doors
simultaneously.

"His Highness,"
he said, "has just
arrived."

In the same flash the
figure of a man had

passed outside the first window, crossing the sunlit pane like a lighted stage. An instant later he passed at the second window and the many mirrors repainted in successive frames the same eagle profile and marching figure. He was erect and alert, but his hair was white and his complexion of an odd ivory yellow. He had that short, curved Roman nose which generally goes with long, lean cheeks and chin, but these were partly masked by moustache and imperial. The moustache was much darker than the beard, giving an effect slightly theatrical, and he was dressed up to the same dashing part, having a white top hat, an orchid in his coat, a yellow waistcoat and yellow gloves which he flapped and swung as he walked. When he came round to the front door they heard the stiff Paul open it, and heard the new arrival say cheerfully, "Well, you see I have come." The stiff Mr. Paul bowed and answered in his inaudible manner;

for a few minutes their conversation could not be heard. Then the butler said, "Everything is at your disposal;" and the glove-flapping Prince Saradine came gaily into the room to greet them. They beheld once more that spectral scene— five princes entering a room with five doors.

The prince put the white hat and yellow gloves on the table and offered his hand quite cordially.

"Delighted to see you here, Mr. Flambeau," he said. "Knowing you very well by reputation, if that's not an indiscreet remark."

"Not at all," answered Flambeau, laughing. "I am not

sensitive. Very few reputations are gained by unsullied virtue."

The prince flashed a sharp look at him to see if the retort had any personal point; then he laughed also and offered chairs to everyone, including himself.

"Pleasant little place, this, I think," he said with a detached air.

"Not much to do, I fear; but the fishing is really good."

The priest, who was staring at him with the grave stare of a baby, was haunted by some fancy that escaped definition. He looked at the grey, carefully curled hair, yellow white visage, and slim, somewhat foppish figure. These were not unnatural, though perhaps a shade prononcé, like the outfit of a figure behind the footlights. The nameless interest lay in something else, in the very framework of the face; Brown was tormented with a half memory of having seen it somewhere before. The man looked like some old friend of his dressed up.

Then he suddenly remembered the mirrors, and put his fancy down to some psychological effect of that multiplication of human masks.

Prince Saradine distributed his social attentions between his guests with great gaiety and tact. Finding the detective of a sporting turn and eager to employ his holiday, he guided Flambeau and Flambeau's boat down to the best fishing spot in the stream, and was back in his own canoe in twenty minutes to join Father Brown in the library and plunge equally politely into the priest's more philosophic pleasures. He seemed to know a great deal both about the fishing and the books, though of these not the most edifying; he spoke five or six languages, though chiefly the slang of each. He had evidently lived in varied cities and very motley societies, for some of his cheerfullest stories were about gambling hells and opium dens, Australian bushrangers or Italian brigands. Father Brown knew that the once-celebrated Saradine had spent his last few years in almost ceaseless travel, but he had not guessed that the travels were so disreputable or so amusing.

Indeed, with all his dignity of a man of the world, Prince Saradine radiated to such sensitive observers as the priest, a certain atmosphere of the restless and even the unreliable. His face was fastidious, but his eye was wild; he had little nervous tricks, like a man shaken by drink or drugs, and he neither had, nor professed to have, his hand on the helm of household affairs. All these were left to the two old servants, especially to the butler, who was plainly the central pillar of the house. Mr. Paul, indeed, was not so much a butler as a sort of steward or, even, chamberlain; he dined privately, but with almost as much pomp as his master; he was feared by all the servants; and he consulted with the prince decorously, but somewhat unbendingly—rather as if he were the prince's solicitor. The sombre housekeeper was a mere shadow in comparison; indeed, she seemed to efface herself and wait only on the butler, and Brown heard no more of those volcanic whispers which had half told him of the younger brother who blackmailed the elder. Whether the prince was really being thus bled by the absent captain, he could not be certain, but there was something insecure and secretive about Saradine that made the tale by no means incredible.

When they went once

more into the long
hall with the windows
and the mirrors,
yellow evening was
dropping over the
waters and the
willowy banks; and
a bittern sounded in
the distance like an
elf upon his dwarfish
drum. The same
singular sentiment
of some sad and evil
fairyland crossed
the priest's mind
again like a little

grey cloud. "I wish Flambeau were back," he muttered.

"Do you believe in doom?" asked the restless Prince Saradine suddenly.

"No," answered his guest. "I believe in Doomsday."

The prince turned from the window and stared at him in a singular manner, his face in shadow against the sunset. "What do you mean?" he asked.

"I mean that we here are on the wrong side of the tapestry," answered Father Brown. "The things that happen here do not seem to mean anything; they mean something somewhere else. Somewhere else retribution will come on the real offender. Here it often seems to fall on the wrong person."

The prince made an inexplicable noise like an animal; in his shadowed face the eyes were shining queerly. A new and shrewd thought exploded silently in the other's mind. Was there another meaning in Saradine's blend of brilliancy and abruptness? Was the prince—Was he perfectly sane? He was repeating, "The wrong person—the wrong person," many more times than was natural in a social exclamation.

Then Father Brown awoke tardily to a second truth. In the mirrors before him he could see the silent door standing open, and the silent Mr. Paul standing in it, with his usual pallid impassiveness.

"I thought it better to announce at once," he said, with the same stiff respectfulness as of an old family lawyer, "a boat rowed by six men has come to the landing-stage, and there's a gentleman sitting in the stern."

"A boat!" repeated the prince; "a gentleman?" and he rose to his feet.

There was a startled silence punctuated only by the odd noise of the bird in the sedge; and then, before anyone could speak again, a new face and figure passed in profile

round the three
sunlit windows,
as the prince had
passed an hour
or two before.
But except for
the accident that
both outlines were
aquiline, they had
little in common.
Instead of the new
white topper of
Saradine, was a black
one of antiquated or
foreign shape; under
it was a young and

very solemn face, clean shaven, blue about its resolute chin, and carrying a faint suggestion of the young Napoleon. The association was assisted by something old and odd about the whole get-up, as of a man who had never troubled to change the fashions of his fathers. He had a shabby blue frock coat, a red, soldierly looking waistcoat, and a kind of coarse white trousers common among the early Victorians, but strangely incongruous today. From all this old clothes-shop his olive face stood out strangely young and monstrously sincere.

"The deuce!" said Prince Saradine, and

clapping on his white hat he went to the front door himself, flinging it open on the sunset garden.

By that time the new-comer and his followers were drawn up on the lawn like a small stage army. The six boatmen had pulled the boat well up on shore, and were guarding it almost menacingly, holding their oars erect like spears. They were swarthy men, and some of them wore earrings. But one of them stood forward beside the olive-faced young man in the red waistcoat, and carried a large black case of unfamiliar form.

"Your name," said the young man, "is

Saradine?"

Saradine assented rather negligently.

The new-comer had dull, dog-like brown eyes, as different as possible from the restless and glittering grey eyes of the prince. But once again Father Brown was tortured with a sense of having seen somewhere a replica of the face; and once again he remembered the repetitions of the glass-panelled room, and put down the coincidence to that. "Confound this crystal palace!" he muttered. "One sees everything too many times. It's like a dream."

"If you are Prince Saradine," said the young man, "I may tell you that my name is Antonelli."

"Antonelli," repeated the prince languidly. "Somehow I remember the name."

"Permit me to present myself," said the young Italian.

With his left hand he politely took off his old-fashioned top-hat; with his right he caught Prince Saradine so ringing a crack across the face that the white top hat rolled down the steps and one of the blue flower-pots rocked upon its pedestal.

The prince, whatever he was, was evidently not a coward; he sprang at his enemy's throat and almost bore him backwards to the grass. But his enemy extricated himself with a singularly inappropriate air of hurried politeness.

"That is all right," he said, panting and in halting English. "I have insulted. I will give satisfaction. Marco, open the case."

The man beside him with the earrings and the big black case proceeded to unlock it. He took out of it two long Italian rapiers, with splendid steel hilts and blades, which he planted point downwards in the lawn. The strange young man standing facing the entrance with his yellow and vindictive face, the two swords standing up in the turf like two crosses in a cemetery, and the

line of the ranked
towers behind,
gave it all an odd
appearance of
being some barbaric
court of justice.
But everything else
was unchanged, so
sudden had been
the interruption.
The sunset gold
still glowed on the
lawn, and the bittern
still boomed as
announcing some
small but dreadful

destiny.

"Prince Saradine," said the man called Antonelli, "when I was an infant in the cradle you killed my father and stole my mother; my father was the more fortunate. You did not kill him fairly, as I am going to kill you. You and my wicked mother took him driving to a lonely pass in Sicily, flung him down a cliff, and went on your way. I could imitate you if I chose, but imitating you is too vile. I have followed you all over the world, and you have always fled from me. But this is the end of the world—and of you. I have you now, and I give you the chance you never gave my father. Choose one of those swords."

Prince Saradine, with contracted brows, seemed to hesitate a moment, but his ears were still singing with the blow, and he sprang forward and snatched at one of the hilts. Father Brown had also sprung forward, striving to compose the dispute; but he soon found his personal presence made matters worse. Saradine was a French freemason and a fierce atheist, and a priest moved him by the law of contraries. And for the other man neither priest nor layman moved him at all. This young man with the Bonaparte face and the brown eyes was something far sterner than a puritan—a pagan. He was a simple slayer from the morning of the earth; a man of the stone age—a man of stone.

One hope remained, the summoning of the household; and Father Brown ran back into the house. He found, however, that all the under servants had been given a holiday ashore by the autocrat Paul, and that only the sombre Mrs. Anthony moved uneasily about the long rooms. But the moment she turned a ghastly face upon him, he resolved one of the riddles of the house of mirrors. The heavy brown eyes of Antonelli were the heavy brown eyes of Mrs. Anthony; and in a flash he saw half the story.

"Your son is outside," he said without wasting words; "either he or the prince will be killed. Where is Mr. Paul?"

"He is at the landing-stage," said the woman faintly. "He is—he is—signalling for help."

"Mrs. Anthony," said Father Brown

seriously, "there is no time for nonsense. My friend has his boat down the river fishing. Your son's boat is guarded by your son's men. There is only this one canoe; what is Mr. Paul doing with it?"

"Santa Maria! I do not know," she said; and swooned all her length on the matted floor.

Father Brown lifted her to a sofa, flung a pot of water over her, shouted for help, and then rushed down to the landing-stage of the little island. But the canoe was already in mid-stream, and old Paul was pulling and pushing it up the river with an energy incredible at his years.

"I will save my master," he cried, his eyes blazing maniacally. "I will save him yet!"

Father Brown could do nothing but gaze after the boat as it struggled up-stream and pray that the old man might waken the little town in time.

"A duel is bad enough," he muttered, rubbing

up his rough dust-coloured hair, "but there's something wrong about this duel, even as a duel. I feel it in my bones. But what can it be?"

As he stood staring at the water, a wavering mirror of sunset, he heard from the other end of the island garden a small but unmistakable sound—the cold concussion of steel. He turned his head.

Away on the farthest cape or headland of the long islet, on a strip of turf beyond the last rank of roses, the duellists had already crossed swords. Evening above them was a dome of virgin gold, and, distant as they were, every detail was picked out. They had cast off their coats, but the yellow waistcoat and white hair of Saradine, the red waistcoat and white trousers of Antonelli, glittered in the level light like the colours of the dancing clockwork dolls. The two swords sparkled from point to pommel like two diamond pins. There was something frightful in the two figures appearing so little and so gay. They looked like two butterflies trying to pin each other to a cork.

Father Brown ran as hard as he could, his little legs going like a wheel. But when he came to the field of combat he found he was born too late and too early—too late to stop the strife, under the shadow of the grim Sicilians leaning on their oars, and too early to anticipate any disastrous issue of it. For the two men were singularly well matched, the prince using his skill with a sort of cynical confidence, the Sicilian using his with a murderous care. Few finer fencing matches

can ever have been
seen in crowded
amphitheatres than
that which tinkled
and sparkled on that
forgotten island
in the reedy river.
The dizzy fight was
balanced so long that
hope began to revive
in the protesting
priest; by all common
probability Paul must
soon come back with
the police. It would
be some comfort

even if Flambeau came back from his fishing, for Flambeau, physically speaking, was worth four other men. But there was no sign of Flambeau, and, what was much queerer, no sign of Paul or the police. No other raft or stick was left to float on; in that lost island in that vast nameless pool, they were cut off as on a rock in the Pacific.

Almost as he had
the thought the
ringing of the rapiers
quickened to a rattle,
the prince's arms
flew up, and the
point shot out behind
between his shoulder-
blades. He went over
with a great whirling
movement, almost
like one throwing
the half of a boy's
cart-wheel. The

sword flew from his hand like a shooting star, and dived into the distant river. And he himself sank with so earth-shaking a subsidence that he broke a big rose-tree with his body and shook up into the sky a cloud of red earth—like the smoke of some heathen sacrifice. The Sicilian had made blood-offering to the ghost of his father.

The priest was instantly on his knees by the corpse; but only to make too sure that it was a corpse. As he was still trying some last hopeless tests he heard for the first time voices from farther up the river, and saw a police boat shoot up to the landing-stage, with constables and other important people, including the excited Paul. The little priest rose with a distinctly dubious grimace.

"Now, why on earth," he muttered, "why on earth couldn't he have come before?"

Some seven minutes later the island was occupied by an invasion of townsfolk and police, and the latter had put their hands on the victorious duellist, ritually reminding him that anything he said might be used against him.

"I shall not say anything," said the monomaniac, with a wonderful and peaceful face. "I shall never say anything more. I am very happy, and I only want to be hanged."

Then he shut his mouth as they led him away, and it is the strange but certain truth that he never opened it again in this world, except to say "Guilty" at his trial.

Father Brown had stared at the suddenly crowded garden, the arrest of the man of blood,

the carrying away
of the corpse after
its examination by
the doctor, rather
as one watches the
break-up of some
ugly dream; he was
motionless, like a
man in a nightmare.
He gave his name
and address as a
witness, but declined
their offer of a boat
to the shore, and
remained alone in the
island garden, gazing

at the broken rose bush and the whole green theatre of that swift and inexplicable tragedy. The light died along the river; mist rose in the marshy banks; a few belated birds flitted fitfully across.

Stuck stubbornly in his sub-consciousness (which was an unusually lively one) was an unspeakable certainty that there was something still unexplained. This sense that had clung to him all day could not be fully explained by his fancy about "looking-glass land." Somehow he had not seen the real story, but some game or masque. And yet people do not get hanged or run through the body for the sake of a charade.

As he sat on the steps of the landing-stage ruminating he grew conscious of the tall, dark streak of a sail coming silently down the shining river, and sprang to his feet with such a backrush of feeling that he almost wept.

"Flambeau!" he cried, and shook his friend

by both hands again and again, much to the astonishment of that sportsman, as he came on shore with his fishing tackle. "Flambeau," he said, "so you're not killed?"

"Killed!" repeated the angler in great astonishment. "And why should I be killed?"

"Oh, because

nearly everybody else is," said his companion rather wildly. "Saradine got murdered, and Antonelli wants to be hanged, and his mother's fainted, and I, for one, don't know whether I'm in this world or the next. But, thank God, you're in the same one." And he took the bewildered Flambeau's arm.

As they turned from the landing-stage they came under the eaves of the low bamboo house, and looked in through one of the windows, as they had done on their first arrival. They beheld a lamp-lit interior well calculated to arrest their eyes. The table in the long dining-room had been laid for dinner when Saradine's destroyer had fallen like a stormbolt on the island. And the dinner was now in placid progress, for Mrs. Anthony sat somewhat sullenly at the foot of the table, while at the head of it was Mr. Paul, the major domo, eating and drinking of the best, his bleared, bluish eyes standing queerly out of his face, his gaunt countenance inscrutable, but by no means devoid of satisfaction.

With a gesture of powerful impatience, Flambeau rattled at the window, wrenched it open, and put an indignant head into the lamp-lit room.

"Well," he cried. "I can understand

you may need some refreshment, but really to steal your master's dinner while he lies murdered in the garden—"

"I have stolen a great many things in a long and pleasant life," replied the strange old gentleman placidly; "this dinner is one of the few things I have not stolen. This dinner and this house and garden happen to belong to me."

A thought flashed across Flambeau's face. "You mean to say," he began, "that the will of Prince Saradine—"

"I am Prince Saradine," said the old man, munching a salted almond.

Father Brown, who

was looking at the birds outside, jumped as if he were shot, and put in at the window a pale face like a turnip.

"You are what?" he repeated in a shrill voice.

"Paul, Prince Saradine, A vos ordres," said the venerable person politely, lifting a glass of sherry. "I

live here very quietly,
being a domestic kind
of fellow; and for
the sake of modesty
I am called Mr. Paul,
to distinguish me
from my unfortunate
brother Mr. Stephen.
He died, I hear,
recently—in the
garden. Of course,
it is not my fault
if enemies pursue
him to this place.
It is owing to
the regrettable

irregularity of his life. He was not a domestic character."

He relapsed into silence, and continued to gaze at the opposite wall just above the bowed and sombre head of the woman. They saw plainly the family likeness that had haunted them in the dead man. Then his old shoulders began to heave and shake a little, as if he were choking, but his face did not alter.

"My God!" cried Flambeau after a pause, "he's laughing!"

"Come away," said Father Brown, who was quite white. "Come away from this house of hell. Let us get into an honest boat again."

Night had sunk on rushes and river by the time they had pushed off from the island, and they went down-stream in the dark, warming themselves with two big cigars that glowed like crimson ships' lanterns. Father Brown took his cigar out of his mouth and said:

"I suppose you can

guess the whole story now? After all, it's a primitive story. A man had two enemies. He was a wise man. And so he discovered that two enemies are better than one."

"I do not follow that," answered Flambeau.

"Oh, it's really simple," rejoined his friend. "Simple, though anything but innocent. Both the Saradines were scamps, but the prince, the elder, was the sort of scamp that gets to the top, and the younger, the captain, was the sort that sinks to the bottom. This squalid officer fell from beggar to blackmailer, and one ugly day he got his hold upon his brother, the prince. Obviously it was for no light matter, for Prince Paul Saradine was frankly 'fast,' and had no reputation to lose as to the mere sins of society. In plain fact, it was a hanging matter, and Stephen literally had a rope round his brother's neck. He had somehow discovered the truth about the Sicilian affair, and could prove that Paul murdered old Antonelli in the mountains. The captain raked in the hush money heavily for ten years, until even the prince's splendid fortune began to look a little foolish.

"But Prince Saradine bore another burden besides his blood-sucking brother. He knew that the son of Antonelli, a mere child at the time of the murder, had been trained in savage Sicilian loyalty, and lived only to avenge his father, not with the gibbet (for he lacked Stephen's legal proof), but with the old weapons of vendetta. The boy had practised arms with a deadly perfection, and about the time that he was old enough to use them Prince Saradine began, as the society papers said, to travel. The fact is that he began to flee for his life, passing from place to place like a hunted criminal; but with one relentless man upon his trail. That was Prince Paul's position, and by no means a pretty one. The more money he spent on eluding Antonelli the less he had to silence Stephen. The more he gave to silence Stephen the less chance there was of finally escaping Antonelli. Then it was that he showed himself a great man—a genius like Napoleon.

"Instead of resisting his two antagonists,

he surrendered
suddenly to both
of them. He gave
way like a Japanese
wrestler, and his foes
fell prostrate before
him. He gave up the
race round the world,
and he gave up his
address to young
Antonelli; then he
gave up everything
to his brother. He
sent Stephen money
enough for smart
clothes and easy

travel, with a letter saying roughly: 'This is all I have left. You have cleaned me out. I still have a little house in Norfolk, with servants and a cellar, and if you want more from me you must take that. Come and take possession if you like, and I will live there quietly as your friend or agent or anything.' He knew that the Sicilian had never seen the Saradine brothers save, perhaps, in pictures; he knew they were somewhat alike, both having grey, pointed beards. Then he shaved his own face and waited. The trap worked. The unhappy captain, in his new clothes, entered the house in triumph as a prince, and walked upon the Sicilian's sword.

"There was one hitch, and it is to the honour of human nature. Evil spirits like Saradine often blunder by never expecting the virtues of mankind. He took it for granted that the Italian's blow, when it came, would be dark, violent and nameless, like the blow it avenged; that the victim would be knifed at night, or shot from behind a hedge, and so die without speech. It was a bad minute for Prince Paul when Antonelli's chivalry proposed a formal duel, with all its possible explanations. It was then that I found him putting off in his boat with wild eyes. He was fleeing, bareheaded, in an open boat before

Antonelli should learn who he was.

"But, however agitated, he was not hopeless. He knew the adventurer and he knew the fanatic. It was quite probable that Stephen, the adventurer, would hold his tongue, through his mere histrionic pleasure in playing a part, his lust for clinging to his new cosy quarters, his rascal's trust in luck, and his fine fencing. It was certain that Antonelli, the fanatic, would hold his tongue, and be hanged without telling tales of his family. Paul hung about on the river till he knew the fight was over. Then he roused the town, brought the police, saw his two vanquished enemies taken away forever, and sat down smiling to his dinner."

"Laughing, God help us!" said Flambeau with a strong shudder. "Do they get such ideas from Satan?"

"He got that idea from you," answered the priest.

"God forbid!" ejaculated Flambeau. "From me! What do you mean!"

The priest pulled a visiting-card from his pocket and held it up in the faint glow of his cigar; it was scrawled with green ink.

"Don't you remember his original invitation to you?" he asked, "and the compliment to your criminal exploit? 'That trick of yours,' he says, 'of getting one detective to arrest the other'? He has just copied your trick. With an enemy on each side of him, he slipped swiftly out of the way and let them collide and kill each other."

Flambeau tore Prince Saradine's card from

the priest's hands and rent it savagely in small pieces.

"There's the last of that old skull and crossbones," he said as he scattered the pieces upon the dark and disappearing waves of the stream; "but I should think it would poison the fishes."

The last gleam of white card and green

ink was drowned and darkened; a faint and vibrant colour as of morning changed the sky, and the moon behind the grasses grew paler. They drifted in silence.

"Father," said Flambeau suddenly, "do you think it was all a dream?"

The priest shook his head, whether in dissent or

agnosticism, but remained mute. A smell of hawthorn and of orchards came to them through the darkness, telling them that a wind was awake; the next moment it swayed their little boat and swelled their sail, and carried them onward down the winding river to happier places and the homes of harmless men.

THE END

ABOUT THE AUTHOR

G.K. Chesteron was an English writer, poet, philosopher, journalist, orator, lay theologian, biographer, and critic. He wrote around 80 books, several hundred poems, some 200 short stories, 4000 essays, and several plays. He had a tendency to forget where he was supposed to be going and miss the train that was supposed to take him there. It is reported that on several occasions he sent a telegram to his wife Frances from some distant (and incorrect) location, writing such things as "Am in Market Harborough. Where ought I to be?" to which she would reply, "Home".

MORE BOOKS AT:

superlargeprint.com

KEEP ON READING!

OBLIGATORY TINY PRINT: This story is in the public domain and published here under fair use laws. The Super Large Print logo is copyright of Super Large Print. The cover design may not be reproduced for commercial purposes. If you have questions or believe we've made a mistake, please let us know at superlargeprint@gmail.com. And thank you for helping this book find it's way to a person who might appreciate it.

This book is set in a font designed by Abelardo Gonzalez called OpenDyslexic

ISBN 9781082768286

Printed in Great Britain
by Amazon

56262372R00086